THE
ABSOLUTELY

AWFUL

MORDICAI GERSTEIN

Voyager Books
Harcourt, Inc.
San Diego   New York   London

www.harcourt.com

First Voyager Books edition 2001
    Voyager Books is a trademark of Harcourt, Inc., registered
        in the United States of America and/or other jurisdictions.

The Library of Congress has cataloged the hardcover edition as follows:
Gerstein, Mordicai.
    The absolutely awful alphabet/Mordicai Gerstein.
        p.   cm.
Summary: An alliterative alphabet book presents mean and
    monstrous letters, from A (an awfully arrogant amphibian) to Z
        (a zigzagging zoological zany).
    1. English language—Alphabet—Juvenile literature.   [1. Alphabet.]   I. Title.
    PE1155.G47   1999
        428.1—dc21   97-40836
            ISBN 0-15-201494-2
                ISBN 0-15-216343-3 pb

H G F E D C B A

The illustrations in this book were done
    in oil paints with pen-and-ink on Opalux Vellum paper.
The display and text type were set in Adroit Medium.
    Color separations by Bright Arts Ltd., Hong Kong
Manufactured by South China Printing Company, Ltd., China
    This book was printed on Arctic matte paper.
Production supervision by Sandra Grebenar and Wendi Taylor
    Designed by Camilla Filancia

For my winningly wonderful wife, Susan, with wuv

**is an
awfully arrogant
Amphibian
annoyed at . . .**

who is a
bashful, belching
Bumpkin
bullied by...

a cruel,
cantankerous
Carnivore
craving to consume…

a dreadfully
dangerous, drooling
Demon
delighted by...

who is extremely
Evil
and eager to
exterminate…

a frightfully
ferocious
Fiend
who favors flattening…

who is
grotesquely
Ghastly
but looks gorgeous next to...

who is
hideously
Horrible
and hates…

an
impossible
Ignoramus
irritated by...

a jolly
jabbering
Joker
who jeers at...

the
knuckleheaded
Knave
who knocked down...

a lanky,
lazy
Loony
in love with...

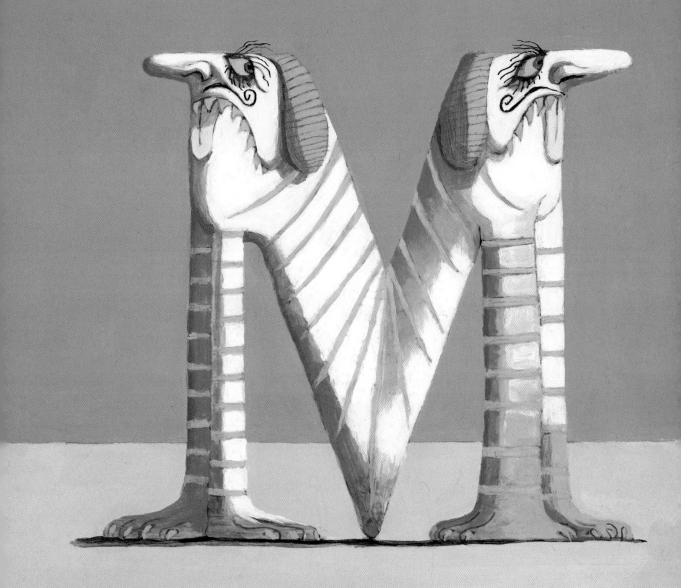

a malicious
mealy-mouthed
Monstrosity
mad at…

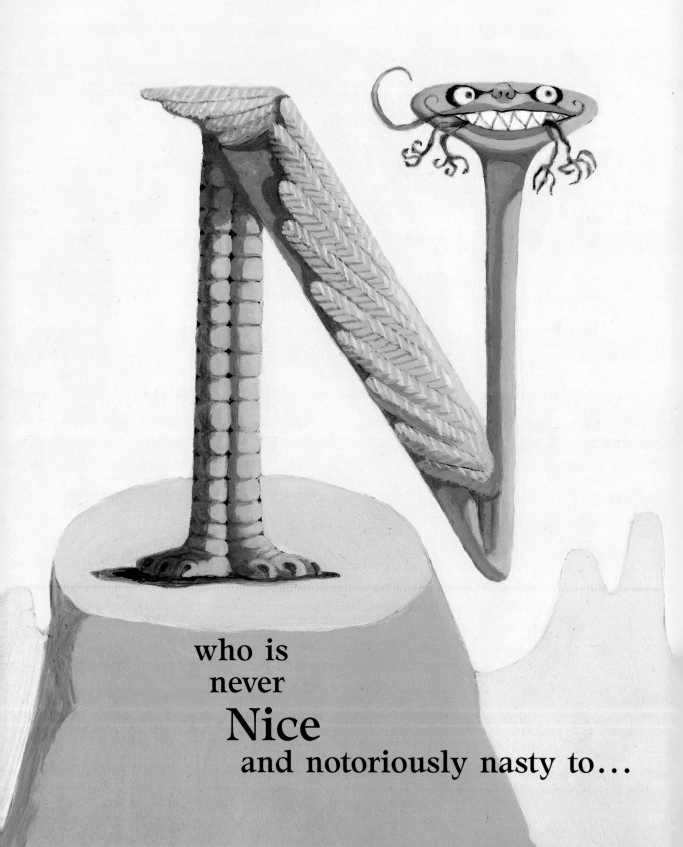

who is
never
Nice
and notoriously nasty to…

an
obnoxious
Oaf
whose odor offends...

a particularly
putrid
Predator
who plans to pulverize...

a quivering,
quizzical
Quacker
who quarrels with...

a rude,
rotten
Ruffian
who ridicules…

a slimy,
spineless
Slob
who sneers at...

a terribly
tedious
Trickster
who teases…

who is
unbelievably
Unpleasant
and utterly unbearable to...

a voracious
vegetable
Vampire
who is viciously vile to…

a wild,
witty
Wacko
who waltzes with . . .

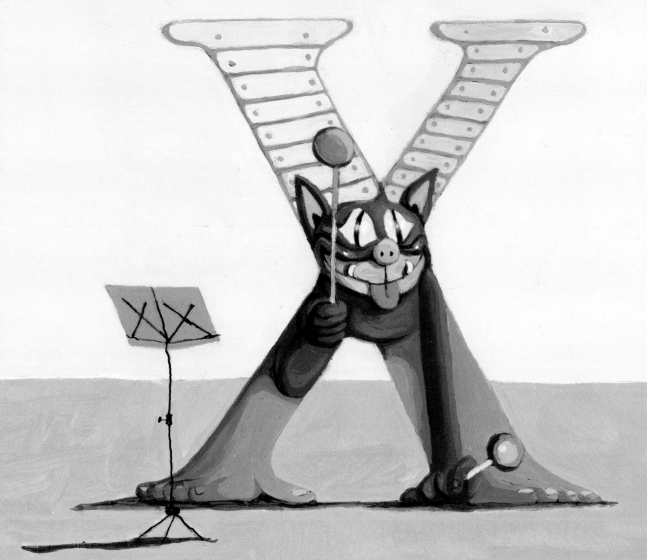

a xeroxing
Xylophonist
longing to
x-ray…

a yucky
young
Yokel
who yodels for...

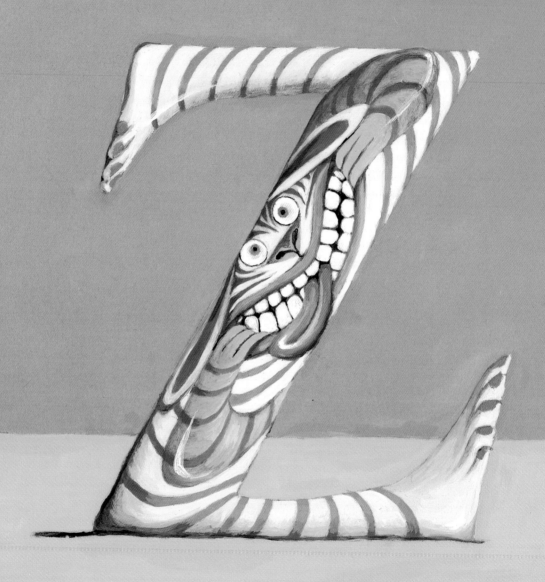

a zigzagging
zoological
ZANY
!